This Little Tiger book belongs to:

Risha

With love on my

birthday From krisha.

xx

For Annie
~A M

For the Farmhouse Mice
~T W

LITTLE TIGER PRESS
1 The Coda Centre, 189 Munster Road, London SW6 6AW
www.littletiger.co.uk

First published in Great Britain 2002
This edition published in 2016
Text copyright © Alan MacDonald 2002
Illustrations copyright © Tim Warnes 2002
Visit Tim Warnes at www.ChapmanandWarnes.com
Alan MacDonald and Tim Warnes
have asserted their rights to be identified
as the author and illustrator of this
work under the Copyright, Designs
and Patents Act, 1988

10 9 8 7 6 5 4 3 2 1

SCAREDY MOUSE

Alan
MACDONALD

★ ★ ★

Tim
WARNES

LITTLE TIGER PRESS
London

In a small hole behind a
cupboard under the stairs lived
a large family of mice.
The youngest was called Squeak.
Squeak was a small mouse,
a scared mouse,
a stay-at-home mouse.

Squeak!

One evening, Squeak was woken up
by his sister, Nibbles.
"Let's go to the kitchen," she said.
"I've just seen something yummy.
A chocolate cake as big as a wheel."

Squeak loved chocolate, but he was very scared.

"What if I get lost?" he worried. "What if we meet the big ginger cat with green eyes?"

"The ginger cat's asleep," said Nibbles. "And I know how to stop you getting lost."

Nibbles fetched a big ball of string,
and tied one end round Squeak.
"There," she said. "All you have to
do is to follow the string and you'll
find your way home."

They scurried out of the mousehole,
and into the dark, shadowy hall.
Squeak kept close to Nibbles, trailing
the string behind him. But as they crossed
the hall, Squeak saw a long, stripy tail.

"IT'S THE CAT, IT'S THE CAT!"
he cried.
Squeak ran this way and that,
harum-scarum, round and back.
"Don't be silly," said Nibbles . . .

Squeak slowly came out of his hiding place.

Through the dining room scampered Nibbles and Squeak. Under the table and under the chairs. But just as Squeak was about to eat a biscuit crumb, he saw two eyes gleaming in the dark.

"IT'S THE CAT, IT'S THE CAT!"
he cried.
Squeak ran this way and that,
harum-scarum, round and back.
"Don't be silly," said Nibbles . . .

Squeak smiled nervously.

Into the lounge they stole, past the
fireplace, and past the ticking clock.
　　Suddenly, Squeak froze in his tracks.
There, peeping above the arm of the
sofa, was a head with two sharp ears.

"IT'S THE CAT, IT'S THE CAT!"
he cried.
Squeak ran this way and that,
harum-scarum, round and back.
"Don't be silly," said Nibbles . . .

"Phew!" sighed Squeak.

Just then, Nibbles spotted the chocolate cake on the table. It didn't take them long to find their way up to it. Soon their paws and whiskers were licky and sticky with chocolate.

"IT'S THE CAT, IT'S THE CAT!"
he cried.
Squeak ran this way and that,
harum-scarum, round and back.
"Don't be silly," said Nibbles . . .

It's only a cushion!

"Silly me!" said Squeak.

Into the kitchen tiptoed the two mice,
across the floorboards and past the cupboard.
Squeak peeped inside.

He shivered and shook. There, in the
shadows, was something furry.

"IT'S THE CAT,
IT'S THE CAT!"
he cried.
Squeak ran this way
and that, harum-scarum,
round and back.
"Don't be silly," said
Nibbles . . .

"Phew!" sighed Squeak.

Just then, Nibbles spotted the chocolate cake on the table. It didn't take them long to find their way up to it. Soon their paws and whiskers were licky and sticky with chocolate.

"Yum," sighed Nibbles. "I could eat all day."
Squeak was a hungry mouse,
but also a worried mouse,
a scared mouse,
a want-to-go-home mouse.

So Nibbles scrambled
down the fridge . . .

and Squeak and the
cake followed.

They heaved the
cake across the
floor, but . . .

just as they reached the door,
a shadow fell across their path.
"IT'S THE CAT, IT'S THE CAT!"
cried Squeak.
"Don't be silly," said Nibbles.
"It's only . . ."

Squeak ran this way and that,
harum-scarum, round and back.
The big ginger cat narrowed his eyes,
opened his claws and . . .

EEEK!

. . . pounced.

But the cat found himself caught in
a web of string. The more he struggled,
the more he became tangled . . .

until soon he was tied up
like a fat ginger parcel.
A mad cat,
a sad cat,
a feeling-a-fool cat.

Squeak was no longer a small or a scared mouse.
He was a bold-as-a-lion mouse.

And the next time he met the
big ginger cat, he just said . . .